SALUTE —— TO SINGING

# SALUTE — TO SINGING

## ONE HUNDRED VARIATIONS
## ON THEMES FROM FOLK-SONGS
## OF THE VOLGA REGION

❀

*Gennady Aygi*

❀

TRANSLATED FROM THE RUSSIAN
BY PETER FRANCE

ZEPHYR PRESS
Brookline, MA

Grateful acknowledgment is due to Akros Books, Kirkcaldy, who
published a bilingual edition of Part One in 1995.

Cover design and illustrations throughout the text are taken from
embroideries by Rose France.
Book design by *typeslowly*
Printed in Canada

Zephyr Press acknowledges with gratitude the financial support
of the Tiny Tiger Foundation, Charles Merrill, the Massachusetts
Cultural Council, and the National Endowment for the Arts.

MASSACHUSETTS CULTURAL COUNCIL

NATIONAL
ENDOWMENT
FOR THE ARTS

*Library of Congress Control Number:* 2002106734

06 05 04 03 02     98765432 FIRST EDITION

ZEPHYR PRESS
50 Kenwood Street
Brookline, MA 02446
www.zephyrpress.org

# INTRODUCTION

Gennady Aygi was born in 1934 in the Chuvash village of Shaymurzino. Even today, while modern in many respects, the village retains much of its ancient character: fertile "black earth," forests, ravines, wooden houses, flocks of geese, a cemetery where the poet's grandfather (the last pagan priest) is buried, hospitable people who speak Chuvash more readily than Russian. Such was the village I visited for the first time in Gennady's company in 1989.

The Chuvash are descended from the Huns of Attila and the ancient Bulgars. They number nearly two million, living mostly on the great bend of the Volga near Kazan. Across the Volga, in Tatarstan, live the more numerous and powerful Tatars, while further north live the Mari and the Udmurt. Each of these peoples has its own language, predominantly Turkic for the Tatars and the Chuvash, Finno-Ugrian for the Mari and the Udmurt, and its own culture. Although there are those who dream of an independent union of the peoples of the Volga, these peoples currently all form separate republics within the Russian Federation.

The Chuvash, Tatars, Mari and Udmurt are all different then, but their songs, collected by folklorists and music-ologists over the last two centuries, have many common elements relating to a shared peasant culture. This is what has enabled the Chuvash poet Gennady Aygi to bring them together as sources for this collection of lyrical "variations." In the southern part of Chuvashia, where the poet grew up, Chuvash and Tatars in particular lived side by side, practicing different religions (the Tatars Islam, the Chuvash Christianity) and speaking different languages, but often intermarrying and living in harmony — or so it seemed when I first went to the country in 1989 and was able to visit a small-town printing house where Chuvash and Tatar editions of the same newspaper were produced in the same building.

Aygi's principal source of inspiration is naturally his own Chuvash culture. The Chuvash, with their Turkic language and pagan religion, were only gradually and incompletely Russified and Christianised in the centuries following their "alliance" with Ivan the Terrible in 1551. Even before this, under the Golden Horde, they had had to retreat into the dark places to preserve their culture. "Chuvash song was a song from the ravine," wrote the musician Kheveder Pavlov. But the culture survived and flowered again, with a new alphabet, in the late nineteenth and early twentieth centuries, when the preservation of the old and the creation of the new often went hand in hand. Now, at the beginning of the twenty-first century, although the break-up of the

Soviet Union has allowed Chuvash national identity to be reasserted, the culture and particularly the language have to be defended in Chuvashia as elsewhere against the power of a larger neighbor.

About 100 years ago, when rural Chuvash culture still survived in an unselfconscious way, the Russian writer N. G. Garin-Mikhailovsky described a Chuvash festival in honour of the God, Tura:

> Coming up to me, the girls joined hands, made a big circle and began to sing; there was something extremely original about their singing, and it was a sight such as I had never seen before.... The big circle went round smoothly and slowly: the girls walked one behind the other, turning sideways, they took one large stride, stopped, and then gently brought the other foot forward....
>
> They looked in front of them and sang.
>
> "What are they singing about?"
>
> "They are singing without words," answered the old man. "This song can only be sung once a year, no more. This is how they will sing when they go to Tura after they die. They will look him in the eyes and will go forward singing ... singing, but without words."
>
> The old man talked, and I listened to him.
>
> Sometimes the sound of the singing grew loud in the fragrant meadows and rose into the sky, mingling with the singing of a lark, a quiet sweet song of times past....

The girls had finished dancing, and they were gazing at me, still enveloped in their song. I came to myself again and in answer to their bow, deeply moved by their greeting and by respect and gratitude, I bowed to them. And transfixed by the song, I could see what is hidden from mortal men.

The last three sentences are the epigraphs chosen by Aygi for his three books of variations on folk songs; they speak for his own situation in relation to his ancestral culture; loving, yet no longer fully belonging.

The son of a teacher of Russian, he early on developed a passion for poetry, both Chuvash and Russian, which took him at the age of twenty to the Gorky Literary Institute in Moscow. Here, although he met with all kinds of trouble because of his friendship with Pasternak and his own unorthodox literary views, he made friends with the young writers and artists who made up the underground culture (another "song from the ravine") of the 1960s and 1970s. Encouraged by Pasternak, he went over to writing poetry in his second language, Russian — and by the 1970s was being recognized throughout Europe as a leading Russian poet, one of the few modern heirs of the great poetic avant-garde of the early twentieth century.

All of this took him away from his native culture. He was writing in a world language, and his points of reference were figures such as Baudelaire, Nietzsche, Kafka, Malevich and Plato. His literary unorthodoxy led to harassment from the authorities in Chuvashia, and the Moscow underground was an essential support system if he was to pursue his lonely task of creating (in an official vacuum) the body of poetry which in Russia only came to be recognised at its true worth in the 1990s.

All the time, though, he remained inwardly inseparable from Chuvashia. While avoiding the easy "folklorism" of the regional writer, he continued to draw from the well of ancestral images: field, forest, clearing, snow. He drew inspiration from the values of the old culture; for him as for his pagan forebears, poetry was a "sacred rite" which creates or maintains a community among people or between human beings and the world they live in. Increasingly, in recent years, he has been reasserting his rootedness in the native land where he is now regarded as the national poet.

In particular, while translating into Chuvash the poetry of several countries, Aygi assembled an anthology of Chuvash poetry, which has been translated into many European languages (the English version, *An Anthology of Chuvash Poetry*, was published in London by Forest Books in 1991). The brief poems of *Salute – to Singing* are variations on some of the vast mass of material that went into the anthology. From early on, Aygi had occasionally written poems based on folk-songs — several of them are included in *Veronica's Book* (Polygon, Edinburgh, 1991) — but in the present collection for the first time he writes more or less explicitly of his relation to the ancient tradition, of love and of loss.

These little poems are indeed Russian variations on Chuvash and occasionally Tatar, Mari, and Udmurt originals. Ideally they should be read alongside the Chuvash anthology. Here, to give a taste of this folk-poetry, is a "guest song" which is echoed in more than one of Aygi's quatrains:

> Oh, the blue flower, deep in the forest!
> Its crown breaks open, and its sound
> Completes the forest's fullness.
> Oh father and mother of ours,
> We come before you and greet you,
> Completing the fullness of the house.
>
> Oh mother, you are a skein of silk!
> A skein of silken threads!
> When we come, you unwind yourself,
> And then, when we go on our way,
> You wind yourself up again.

Peter France<br>Edinburgh, March 2001

*to my daughter Veronica*

SALUTE — TO SINGING

...закончив, они смотрели на меня,
охваченные своей песней.

*Н. Гарин-Михайловский*

PART ONE

THIRTY-SIX VARIATIONS
ON THEMES FROM CHUVASH
AND TATAR FOLK-SONGS
(1988-1991)

". . . they had finished, and they were gazing at me,
still enveloped in their song."

*N. Garin-Mikhailovsky*

1.

Золотая проволока — фигура твоя,
о, из алого мельканья
лицо,
выше — шелковый воздух.


2.

Был конь у меня, —
хоть растянись ты на нем и поспи!
На крупе могла, не расплескиваясь,
держаться вода.


3.

Мама в гости меня отпустила,
чтоб я покачивалась,
словно жертвенный котел над огнем,
в пеньи — пред вами.

1.

Golden wire your shape,
oh, a face
of shimmering scarlet,
above it — silky air.

2.

Once I had a horse —
you could stretch out on him and sleep!
Water could lie on his back
and not a drop spill.

3.

Mother let me go visiting
to stand here and rock
like a ritual pot on the fire
singing — before you.

4.

В доме у батюшки
медным огнем освещает лучина,
все равно занимаюсь: золотом горит рукоделье!
Не надо чужого огня серебряного.

5.

А тень ее там, все за той же оградой,
завтра пойдешь — не застанешь,
тогда-то в тебя
войдет навсегда ее облик.

6.

Стан мой — фигура татарская!
Видимо, слишком разошлась среди вас, —
в пляске очертанья она растеряла
фигуры татарской.

4.

In our old father's home
a spill sheds copper light,
but still I keep working: my handwork gleams gold!
no need for strange silver lamplight.

5.

And her shadow is there, still behind the fence,
go there tomorrow, you won't find her,
but then her image
will sink into you forever.

6.

My figure is a Tatar shape!
She must have moved too much among you —
in the dancing she lost the lineaments
of that Tatar shape.

7.

Поплакала ты и притихла,
и теперь одиноко белеешь в сенях,
как шелковая нитка
в ушке игольном.

8.

Вышивки — в танце — на вас!
То ли кланяются васильки,
то ли
щебечут ласточки.

9.

Остановитесь у ворот полевых,
приподыму я колпак мой,
пусть мои кудри еще поблестят вам
в поле родном.

7.

You wept, then fell quiet,
and now shine lonely white in the porch,
like a silken thread
in a needle's ear.

8.

Embroidery — in it you all dance! —
now cornflowers bowing,
and now
swallows twittering.

9.

If you stop by the field gate,
I shall raise my cap,
may my curls again shine on you all
in the fields of home.

10.

Стан мой легкий, глаза мои черные
в этом огне хоровода родного
горят, быть может,
в последний раз.

11.

Не уменьшить мне боль,
полдуши в этом поле оставив!
Молчу я, и лишь за холмом, как ребенок,
громко плачет куница.

12.

Прибыли мы за невестою
с сердцем белым,
сделаем свадьбу
белее снега.

10.

My slender figure, my dark eyes
burn in the fire
of our native dance
for the last time, perhaps.

11.

There's no way to still my pain,
half my soul remains in that field!
I say nothing, but beyond the hill like a child
a marten weeps out loud.

12.

We have come for the bride
with the snow white heart,
let us make a wedding
whiter than snow.

13.

Если запустить мое пенье
ладом скользящим,
лучшая песенка выкатится
клубком золотым.

14.

Кружась все быстрее,
родные остаются луга,
значит, в деревне уже не вмещается
отныне мой тоненький стан.

15.

Что ж ожидании нас
белым полотном не застлали ваш двор?
И монету серебряную не прикрепили
ко лбу вашего дома.

13.

If I set my singing
on a slippery track,
the best song will roll out
like a golden ball.

14.

Turning faster and faster,
the meadows of home fall behind,
and no more my slender figure
will find a place in the village.

15.

Why then as they awaited us
did they not drape their yard in white?
And no silver coin has been nailed
to your house's forehead.

16.

Танцуя,
в бусы превратим кирпичи этой печи,
серебряные в ней загорятся
дрова.


17.

Задрожали
верхушки берез,
как белая луна, появляется
невеста в воротах.


18.

Есть — песенка средь трав на лугу,
пойти ли к ней и запеть ли,
иль принести вам сюда
и спеть — на прощанье?

16.

Dancing,
we shall turn the bricks of this stove to beads
and in it will blaze up
silver logs.

17.

The tops of the birch trees
have started trembling,
like a white moon, the bride
appears at the gate.

18.

Yes, a song amid the meadow grass,
shall we go there and start singing,
or bring it to you here
and sing it in parting.

19.

Вот, уже исчезают
в поле, среди ковылей.
Уже не слышно бубенчиков.
Мы как птицы стоим.

20.

Все настойчивей зов одинокий
иволги — за околицей,
подружки невесты задвигались,
как овсяные снопы золотые.

21.

Голос мой тонкий, как голос кукушки,
ветром потом отнесет
долго звенеть
рядом с оставленным домом.

19.

Look, already they vanish
in the field, among grasses,
no carriage bells now to be heard.
Like birds we stand.

20.

Ever stronger the lonely call
of the oriole outside the village,
the bridesmaids have set out
like sheaves of golden oats.

21.

My voice is soft as the cuckoo's,
it will be carried off by the wind
and echo long
by the abandoned house.

22.

Ах, и золотистые мы, и алые!
Проехав при свете листа кленового,
въезжаем
при свете пшеничной стерни.


23.

Отправилась милая в путь, и черная ласточка
навстречу ночи
мчится — по крыльям лия
ручьи дождевые.


24.

А богата была — девятью походками:
чередовались — играли!
Потом
жизнь оставила — только одну.

22.

Oh, we are golden, we are scarlet!
Riding by in the light of maple leaves,
we come riding in
by the light of wheat stubble.

23.

The beloved set out, and black swallow
flies to meet
the night — pouring from her wings
the streaming rain.

24.

And she was rich — with nine ways of walking
one-after-another in play!
Then life
left her with just the one.

25.

По этому полю проедем
от края до края,
каждый лепесток каждой ромашки
приподымая.

26.

Встречая меня,
отец мой раскатывается, как шелковый тюк,
скатывается обратно,
меня проводив.

27.

Никто, ничего, ни о чем,
так и проходит мой век,
вода течет, — никто не спрашивает:
«Как ты течешь?»

25.

Over this field we shall ride
from one edge to the other,
lifting each single petal
of every daisy.

26.

Coming out to meet me,
my father rolls out like a skein of silk,
and when he has seen me off
he rolls up again.

27.

No one, nothing, to no end,
so my time goes past,
water flows — and no one asks it:
"How do you flow?"

28.

Мама, на подоле твоем
все следы — от подпрыгиваний
детских ножек моих!
Дай, лицом прикоснусь.


29.

Точно конопляное поле отцовское,
ровны лесные вершины,
плывет моя песня над ними,
будто поет это — лес.


30.

В поле — зеленого жаль,
жаль — золотого над полем!
Брат мой, стареем,
седеем, как синие бусы.

28.

Mother on your hem
are the marks — of my skipping
baby feet!
Let me bury my face in it.

29.

Like our father's field of hemp,
the forest tops are level,
over them swims my song
as if the forests were singing.

30.

In the field — pity for the green!
Pity for the gold overhead!
Brother, we are growing old,
going grey like blue beads.

31.

Принесли мы изящество ног,
чтобы
в памяти вашей оставить!
Разрешите нам пляску последнюю.

32.

Давно уж не видно деревни,
а окна отцовского дома
трещинами в рамах свистят,
призывая — вернуться.

33.

Мама, начнешь подметать ты горницу,
может быть, вспомнишь меня,
споткнешься
и перед дверью заплачешь.

31.

We have brought the beauty of legs
so that in your memory
it will remain.
Allow us this one last dance.

32.

The village is long since out of sight,
but the windows in our father's house
whistle through cracks in the frame,
calling us home again.

33.

Mother, you will start sweeping the room,
and remembering me, perhaps,
you will stop short
by the door and burst out crying.

34.

Горит свеча,
не видимая глазу красной лисы,
прощайте, — очертанья души моей юной
пребудут средь вас.

35.

Хватит, покружились мы здесь,
как звонкие монеты серебряные,
поклонимся, — согнемся пред вами,
как белые деньги бумажные.

36.

И там, где стояли мы,
пусть останется
свечение — нашего
благословения.

34.

A candle burns,
unseen by the red fox's eye,
farewell — my young soul's features
will abide among you.

35.

Enough, we have swung and swung
like resounding silver coins,
we shall bow, we shall bend before you,
like paper money, all white.

36.

And where we stood,
may there remain
the shining of our
benediction.

Я пришел в себя и в ответ на их поклон,
проникнутый и сам приветом, уважением
и признательностью, поклонился им.

*Н. Гарин-Михайловский*

PART TWO

THIRTY-SIX VARIATIONS
ON THEMES FROM CHUVASH
AND MARI FOLK-SONGS
(1998-1999)

"I came to myself again and in answer to their bow,
deeply moved by their greeting and by respect and
gratitude, I bowed to them."

*N. Garin-Mikhailovsky*

1.

Вы с нами уже попрощались
и пением, и молчанием грустным!
Но пока что — мы все и полностью
в ваших глазах.

2.

Соломинка на дороге, соломинка,
краса — Земли!
Но сдует ветер, и шуткой
кончится эта краса.

3.

И вновь, призывая
в поле — для нового гула труда,
в небе резвятся
белые кони грозы.

1.

Already you have said goodbye to us
with singing and sad silence!
But for now we are still present
in your eyes completely.

2.

A straw on the road, a straw,
beauty — of the Earth!
But the wind will blow, and this beauty
will end in a jest.

3.

And again, calling us to the field,
to a new surge of work,
the storm's white horses
whinny in the sky.

4.

Дошел ли, внезапно, шепот беды,
тронул ли кто-то, утешая, рукой?
Нет, это просто — ветер откинул
левую полу моего армяка.

5.

И цветущая черемуха
издали
одиноко белеет
будто продвигаясь — сквозь лес.

6.

Только что спели Песнь о Сохе,
и уже на конях
сидим, наблюдая за жаворонком
в небе весеннем.

4.

Is it a sudden whisper of disaster,
or a hand's comforting touch?
No, just the wind flinging back
the left flap of my greatcoat.




5.

And the flowering bird-cherry
from afar
all alone shines white,
as though moving — through the forest.




6.

We have just sung the Song of the Plough,
and now on our horses
we sit and gaze up at the lark
in the spring sky.

7.

Осиротевший, брожу я один,
лежит на лугу олененок,
белый от него подымается пар,
душно весь день от тоски.

8.

Алея, приближается Время Хороводов,
веянье этого — в лесах и лугах;
у входа в деревню, за речкой,
цветы арбуза — как свежие снега.

9.

Крона черемухи —
словно встревоженная ласточек стая:
буря! —
бьются они, не взлетая.

7.

Orphaned, I wander alone,
a fawn is lying in the meadow,
white vapor rises from him,
the whole day is heavy with sorrow.

8.

The Time of Dancing approaches, scarlet,
it is felt in forest and field;
at the entrance to the village by the stream
watermelons flower like fresh snow.

9.

The bird-cherry's crown
seems a startled flock of swallows;
a storm! —
the wings beat, without flying.

10.

Белый — на лугу — расцветает цветок,
— и ты — в рост, и растение — в цвет, —
лу́га — торжество, луга — исполненность,
ай-ийя-юр.




11.

Лишь в сновиденьи войду
в этот наш двор,
тише, любимый мой пес,
рыжий ты мой соловей.




12.

Алый — в саду — расцветает цветок,
— и ты — в рост, и растение — в цвет, —
сада — торжество, сада — исполненность,
ай-ийя-юр.

10.

White – on the meadow — the flower blooms,
— and you at full height, the plant in full flower, —
triumph of the meadow, meadow's fulfillment,
ay-iya-yur.

11.

Only dreaming shall I enter
this courtyard of ours,
hush, my favorite dog,
my russet nightingale.

12.

Red — in the garden — the flower blooms,
— and you at full height, the plant in full flower, —
triumph of the garden, garden's fulfillment,
ay-iya-yur.

13.

Шорох березы — как шепот «прощай»,
а над нею
стриж одинокий —
как падающие ножницы.


14.

Тянутся стада к водопою,
скоро начнется хоровод за селом, —
вся деревня белым-бела
от девичьих нарядов.


15.

Сколько братьев и сверстников — столько красы,
все больше и бездн — их отсутствия!
Голову мою отпускаю на волю —
пусть ищет, чем успокоиться.

13.

The birch's rustle — like a whispered goodbye,
and above it
a solitary swift —
like falling scissors.

14.

The herds are wandering to water,
soon the dance will begin beyond the houses, —
the whole village is white as white
with the maidens' costumes.

15.

So many brothers and friends — such beauty,
even more the abysses of their absence!
I give my head its freedom —
let it seek out a source of comfort.

16.

Мы песнею
отцовский заполнили дом, —
побудьте вы молча, пока удаляемся
в поле ночном.


17.

При пении косарей
вдруг затихаю я с думой
о том, что хорош для наклона в косьбе
юный мой стан.


18.

Вместо серпа, для меня предназначенного,
выкуйте ручку для двери, —
радуйтесь, ее открывая,
закрывая, задумайтесь.

16.

With a song we have filled
the house of our father, —
be quiet now, while we leave
through fields at night.


17.

Hearing the mowers sing,
I grow quiet with the thought
that my young shape is just right
to bend in the mowing.


18.

Instead of a sickle, destined for me,
hammer out a door handle, —
be glad when you open it,
when you close it, be thoughtful.

19.

Все — в белом,
в поле жнецы разбрелись,
как разбросанные серебряные кольца
в золоте ржи.



20.

А после — останется
во снах, да в чужих краях,
платок, поблескивающий
за три версты.



21.

Чтобы кукушка шалила, я не слыхал, —
чтобы, заикаясь, она хохотала!
Видимо, у Бога кончаются
все умные Его времена.

19.

All are in white,
reapers dot the field
like silver rings scattered
in the gold of the rye.


20.

And afterwards there will remain
in dreams and foreign places
a headscarf, gleaming bright
from a league away.


21.

Unheard-of, a cuckoo playing pranks, —
a cuckoo stammering as it laughs!
It must be God seeing the end
of all the times of his wisdom.

22.

И заполняется поле
все более цветеньем гречихи,
с утра дополняемым
пением нашим.


23.

И черные воды
текут, виясь,
прореживая перья в крыле
одинокого гуся.


24.

Начинается пляска,
и свечи зажгите такие,
чтоб озарилась
вся — подруги моей — красота.

22.

And the field is ever fuller
of the buckwheat's flowering,
augmented from early morning
by the sound of our singing.


23.

And the black waters
flow, coiling,
cutting feathers on the wing
of a lonely goose.


24.

The dancing begins,
and you must light such candles
that all — my girl's — beauty
shall be illuminated.

25.

Поля, почерневшие от наших рук,
от них же теперь золотятся,
словно в песне, одной и той же,
загорается по-разному — радость.


26.

Мы — такие цветы луговые!
Если наших головок
девичьи не коснутся подолы,
не откроемся, не распустимся.


27.

Давно тебя нет, но черты-очертанья твои
мелькают, разрозненные, в полях и лесах —
на лицах, на спинах, плечах
правнуков и внуков твоих.

25.

The fields, blackened by our hands,
are now made golden by them,
like joy springing different
in one and the same song.


26.

We are as meadow flowers!
If the maidens' hems
do not touch our heads,
we shall not open, not blossom.


27.

You have long gone, but your features, your outlines
separately shine in the fields, the forests —
in the faces, the backs, the shoulders
of your grandchildren and great-grandchildren.

28.

Мы играем в бусы, а сорока
мимо дома, мимо Алендэя
чертит-чертит крылышком зеленым,
бусы белые бросает Пинерби.

29.

Потом, появившись во сне,
как на мосточек, ты ступишь
на тот же вечерний, на той же тропинке,
гаснущий свет.

30.

Юность — как луг! И, побывшие там,
одно мы запомнили:
игры девушек — это крапива,
игры парней — чертополох.

28.

We play at beads, and the magpie
past the house, Alendei's house,
draws and draws with a green feather,
throws white beads to Pinerbi.


29.

And then, appearing through sleep,
as on to a little bridge,
you step out, along the same path,
on the same dying light of evening.


30.

Youth is like a meadow! And having been there,
one thing we remember:
the girls' games are nettles,
the boys' games are thistles.

**31.**

Будто что-то случилось с жизнью моей!
Ударившись о лесную ограду,
солнце тяжело восходит
из-за редких дубов.


**32.**

А леса начало
в инее таком небывалом:
страшусь и подумать,
как же я в это войду.


**33.**

Мерцая, приближается Праздник Саней
и среди нас опускается,
скоро растаять ему
вместе со снегом последним.

31.

Something has happened to my life!
Rattling the forest fence,
the sun heavily rises
from behind a few oaks.

32.

But the forest's beginning
is in such unheard-of frost:
I tremble just to think
how I can go into it.

33.

Gleaming, the Feast of Sleighs approaches
and settles down among us,
soon to melt away
with the last of the snow.

34.

Вяжу тебе давно рукавицы,
что лопнули мозоли на пальцах,
и глаза испортились, всматриваясь вдаль
в ожиданьи тебя так.



35.

Долог, как горе, мой путь,
и снега почерневшие
давно уж съедают лодыжки
коня моего.



36.

И облако плывет, круглясь,
будто шапка на моей голове,
и век мой проходит, как в сновидении,
без сна увиденном.

34.

I have knitted you mittens for so long
the blisters have split my fingers,
and my eyes are worn out staring
to see if you are on the road.

35.

Long, like grief, is my road,
and the blackened snows
have long been consuming
my horse's ankle-bones.

36.

And a cloud is floating, a round cloud,
like a cap on my head,
and my time passes, like a dream
dreamed without sleep.

И, заколдованный песней, я видел
теперь то, что скрыто от смертных.

*Н. Гарин-Михайловский*

PART THREE

TWENTY-EIGHT VARIATIONS
ON THEMES FROM CHUVASH
AND UDMURT FOLK-SONGS
(1999-2000)

"And transfixed by the song,
I could see what is hidden from mortal men."

*N. Garin-Mikhailovsky*

1.

Давайте встанем в ряд,
подобно ладной ограде,
приосанимся, подобно луне
в пору полнолуния.

2.

Скоро удаляться нам в поле,
скоро и оттуда исчезнуть! —
Соседи и родные, шумя и покачиваясь,
поют, как Елабужский лес.

3.

Увидел огонек — подошел я к окну,
позвал, но ты голову не подняла,
только шелковая пряжа рассыпалась
будто шепотом грустным.

1.

Let us stand all in a line,
like a well-made fence,
let us stand proud, like the moon
at a time of full moon.

2.

Soon we must go out to the field,
soon from there too we shall vanish! —
Neighbors and family, rustling, swaying,
sing like the forest of Yelábuga.

3.

I saw a light — I went up to the window,
I called, but you didn't lift your head,
only the silken threads were strewn
as in a grieving whisper.

4.

Прямо в сиянье мороза
пою я — как другу в лицо,
и от голоса уже индевеет
шубы моей воротник.


5.

И сквозь звезду
виднеется дорога,
по которой уйдем,
чтоб не вернуться.


6.

Когда со двора выходила,
с отцом разлучаясь,
лучше бы шелковой ниткой я стала,
чтоб, зацепившись, остаться.

4.

I sing to the shining of the frost,
as into the face of a friend,
and already my coat collar
is frosted by my voice.

5.

And through the star
the road is seen,
on which we shall go
and not return.

6.

When I was leaving our yard
and parting from my father,
I should have become a silken thread
to cling there and remain.

7.

А сквозь луну
видится поле,
на котором мы
останемся, павшие.

8.

Брат мой, из детства моего,
ушел, как из сказки грустной,
мне снится его старая мельница:
шесть крыльев — как шесть огней.

9.

И, наконец, опустилась
я на колени средь поля,
не оттого, что устала,
а потому, что горела душа.

7.

And through the moon
the field is seen,
on which we shall fall
and there remain.

8.

My brother walked out of my childhood,
as out of a sad story,
I dream of his old mill:
six sails — like six fires.

9.

And at last I fell to my knees
in the middle of the field,
not because I was tired,
but because my soul was burning.

**10.**

В доме от пения то светло, то темно,
будто, от дыхания нашего,
держатся над нами
поляны тепла.

**11.**

А конь вороной ушел,
потому что забыли закрыть ворота,
а с поля, внезапно притихшего,
во двор как будто вошла беда.

**12.**

И вдруг просыпаюсь,
словно — услышав тебя!
Солнце восходит,
вкруг яблони светом виясь.

10.

The singing in the house
makes it dark and then light,
as if from our breathing
glades of light floated above us.


11.

And the black horse went away
because the gate was left open,
and from the field, suddenly hushed,
misfortune seemed to enter the yard.


12.

And suddenly I awake,
as if I heard your voice!
the sun is rising,
its light entwines the apple trees.

13.

Братья уже входят в село
с Песнею в честь Возвращения,
и ветер шумит в горах,
заставляя шалить оленят.


14.

Коснулись ли руки чужие? — трону слегка:
змеей изогнется (значит — притрагивались),
защебечет, как ласточка
(значит — не тронули).


15.

Конь мой понесся быстрее,
ждет, очевидно, меня мой сват,
заранее отворяя ворота, —
деревянный свой семафор.

13.

The brothers are entering the village already,
with a Song to honour the Return,
and the sound of the wind in the hills
sets the young deer playing.

14.

Have other hands touched her? I touch her lightly:
she writhes like a snake (they have touched her),
or she twitters like a swallow
(they haven't).

15.

My horse has begun to gallop,
the matchmaker must be waiting,
opening his gates in advance —
his wooden semaphore.

16.

Грустно, — и погода дождит,
истрепывая старую одежду мою,
и горюющее сердце изношено
плачущею постоянно душой.


17.

Вы настолько покинули
нашу память о вас,
что не возвращаетесь
даже и в наши сны.


18.

Пою я, и будто сквозь слезы
что-то мелькает в гореньи заката, —
это по давнему полю идем
мы с конем вдвоем.

16.

Sadness and falling rain
tousling my old clothes —
and the grieving heart is worn out
by the ever weeping soul.




17.

You have left so far behind
our memory of you
that you do not come back
even into our dreams.




18.

I sing, and as if through tears
something gleams in the fire of sunset —
it is me walking with my horse
alone through the fields of old.

19.

А за туманом
у дуба зелен́ого
нет и посильнее ветки,
чтоб пошуметь.

20.

Неживыми на чужбине останутся
эти руки и эта голова, —
дым паровоза бьет нам в лицо,
чтобы памяти лишить напоследок.

21.

И внезапно — покой, как будто
я, для этого, в мире один,
и вьюга во дворе, вьюга в огороде,
вьюга в полях.

19.

And beyond the mist
the little green oak
has no more than a branch
to rustle with.

20.

Lifeless in foreign lands
these hands and this head will remain —
the engine's smoke blows in our faces
to rob us of future memory.

21.

And suddenly — quietness, as if
for this I was alone in the world,
a blizzard in the yard, in the garden,
a blizzard over the fields.

22.

И день притих, будто умерло
что-то важное в нем,
и спит лиса у подножья горы,
укрывшись красным хвостом.


23.

Меж Казанской землей и Чувашской
видели вы столб межевой?
Это не столб, это я там стою, — от несчастья
одеревенелая.


24.

И очень ярко,
как в русской песне,
ветками перебирает
береза по имени Александр.

22.

And the day has fallen quiet,
as if something important had died,
and the fox sleeps at the foot of the hill,
wrapped up in his red tail.

23.

Between Kazan and the Chuvash lands
have you seen the boundary post?
It isn't a post. I stand there,
turned to wood by misfortune.

24.

And very vividly,
as in a Russian song,
a birch named Alexander
strums its branches.

25.

Смотрю на воду — она спокойна,
и думаю тихую мысль:
можно пережить еще что-то хорошее,
ведь может быть доброй и смерть.

26.

Вдруг все вернулись, все вместе,
но пугающими становятся крики и шум,
и с усилием останавливаю сон,
как в степи останавливают обоз.

27.

И не падают ли пояса с наших талий,
не прошла ли жизнь? —
Спрашиваю так, как кукушка кукует,
как бьют часы.

25.

I look into the water — it is peaceful,
and I think a quiet thought:
I can still see something good,
and death too can be kind.

26.

Suddenly all have returned, all together,
but the shouts and the noise grow frightening,
and I stop the dream with effort,
as they stop a cart in the steppe.

27.

And do the sashes not fall from our waists,
and has life not passed us by? —
I ask, like the cuckoo calling
or a clock striking the hours.

28.

Снова — страда, и певцы и птицы
задумываются и умолкают,
кто-то — на время,
кто-то — быть может — уже навсегда.

28.

Again the work time — singers and birds
grow thoughtful and fall silent,
some for a time,
and some, perhaps, forever.

# IN THE GRIP OF STRANGE THOUGHTS: RUSSIAN POETRY IN A NEW ERA

◆ 118 POEMS BY 32 CONTEMPORARY RUSSIAN POETS

◆ BILINGUAL (RUSSIAN & ENGLISH) ON FACING PAGES

◆ FOREWORD BY POET AND CRITIC MIKHAIL AIZENBERG

◆ INTRODUCTION AND AFTERWORD BY J. KATES

◆ BIOGRAPHICAL NOTES ON POETS AND TRANSLATORS

444 PAGES
0-939010-5-69  19.95 PAPER
0-939010-5-77  30.00 CLOTH

"...an enjoyable and admirable work. Its thirty-two poets show a tremendous thematic and stylistic range, but are united in their feeling for the vitality of language."
—*The Times Literary Supplement*

"This book is an absolute gift to students and to lovers of poetry" —*British East-West Journal*

## ZEPHYR PRESS

617.713.2813 PHONE & FAX
EDITOR@ZEPHYRPRESS.ORG
WWW.ZEPHYRPRESS.ORG